Crescent City Kitty and Bone-A-Part In Faithful Friends

By Robin R. Whaley

Writing and Illustrations Copyright © 2018 Robin R. Whaley

All rights reserved.

This is a work of fiction. Names, characters, businesses, places, events and incidents are either the product of the author's imagination or used in a fictitious manner. Any resemblance to actual persons, living or dead, or actual events is purely coincidental.

Illustrations are mixed media by Robin R. Whaley.

Boneapart Art, LLC

www.boneapartart.com

www.robinwhaley.com

www.crescentcitykittyandboneapart.com

ISBN: 9781729208298

Dedication

This book is dedicated to Laura Long Legs (2005-2016) and The World Trade Center Cats New Orleans.

ACKNOWLEDGMENTS

A Special Thank You to the following people:

Mary Susan Phillips, Omar Abu Staiti, F and F, Kenneth and Ann Taylor, and Mom

I grew up in New Orleans and lived uptown with our family my whole life. We were all happy, but I was searching for a best friend because I felt lost. A little over a year ago, I found the Crescent City* Kitty, and she was adopted by my family. Our lives were fulfilled. Mom and Mr. Bob, our human caretaker when Mom flies, spoil us in every possible way. My fondest memories were spending time in Audubon Park.* We ran through the magnificent, majestic oaks and swam with the Black-bellied Whistling-Ducks* and Red-Eared Sliders* in the ponds. Henry, Faith, and I would swim and Crescent City Kitty would sit with Mom. We may be fur-siblings, but we were also faithful friends.

If the weather were not too hot, sticky, and humid, we would run up and down Monkey Hill* and then watch submarine races at the Fly.* We would not stay out too late because Henry and Faith would chase the nutria* when it turned dusk. Kitty regularly took up for those frightful rodents. I could never understand why she liked the nutria. They are ugly, have big sharp teeth, and parade around with their long rat tails. Every time I would criticize them, Crescent City Kitty would tell me, "Bone-A-Part,* don't judge a book by its cover!"

---

*See Glossary

Kitty often visited with her cat family who lived down the street next door to each other on the corner of Henry Clay* and Tchoupitoulas.* We all hung out and rode up and down the elevator in one of the houses. A yellow-headed Amazon parrot* named Arthur Macaroni who lived in the house with the elevator often talked and whistled to us. The cats and I would laugh when he hung upside down from the chandelier and screamed at the top of his lungs. We loved it when he got too excited and would fall! Even though we enjoyed hanging out with her feline family, we preferred to romp under the Live Oaks in Audubon Park with Henry and Faith.

One day when we were strolling back home from our visit, Kitty and I talked about taking an afternoon trip back to the deserted World Trade Center* where I had met her. Kitty had grown up with the WTC* colony of homeless cats, and we wanted to visit the Ferry Cats, who were her neighbors, and see how they were surviving. She was passionate about feeding homeless animals and could relate to their suffering.

Kitty said, "Let's bring them both moist and dry gluten-free cat food."

We delayed our visit to see Kitty's friends until Mom had flown back down to Latin America on one of her regular trips. Mr. Bob arrived in the mornings and evenings to feed us, so we planned to leave after breakfast and to return before dinner. Mom, who is an air hostess for *FLY Away Airways* and based out of MSY,* was usually away from our home for twenty four hours when she flew to Lima, Peru.*

We did not tell Henry and Faith about our plan to visit with the Ferry Cats; they would have wanted to travel along, and Kitty and I wanted to spend time with each other. I could tell Henry and Faith knew something was different, but they did not say anything at all because they knew Kitty was my best friend.

The food was already packed for the cat colony and we set out on our good deed for the day. Since we were familiar with Tchoupitoulas Street and knew that it ran along the Mississippi River,* I said, "Kitty, all we have to do is follow the river to get downtown!" We walked under the Crescent City Connection and watched a riverboat paddle by.

Kitty and I reminisced about our last adventure from when we had first met and visited the old places we knew along the way. The seagulls and pelicans flew over and greeted us.

Kitty and I visited Jackson Square,* the park I had shown her when we met. Mom would walk me there with Henry and Faith, but Kitty, who lived near the WTC, had never seen it before she found me.

Kitty said, "Bone-A-Part, I am so excited about going back to the place I came from!"

We spent some time playing in the park and hanging out in front of the St. Louis Cathedral.* There was a band playing our favorite song and people of all ages were dancing. They were twirling parasols* and handkerchiefs as they strutted the second line* through the streets of the French Quarter.*

We eventually approached the former World Trade Center, which was the hub of the cats' universe and Kitty's former home.

A single, lonely light was still on in the abandoned building. Kitty looked up at the light and said, "Back when I lived here, I always sensed a presence near me, and it felt like someone was looking out for my well-being. And I still feel it, like there are eyes in the sky watching over me."

Kitty and I wondered who or what lived there, but this mystery would have to wait for another day.

Kitty and I wandered to the Canal Street Ferry Station and found the cats, who had been her neighbors, under the jet way among the many blooming azaleas. The WTC cats and Ferry Cats had been friends for years. We greeted each other, and they were excited to receive the food we had brought for them. Lou, who was the most senior of the Ferry Cats, said, "How is your Momma and them![*] Tell her we said, 'Thank You'!"

After spending time together, Kitty and I decided to make our way back home. We still had plenty of time at this point to return home before dinner. However, as we departed, I saw several signs. They stated in bold, red letters that construction would resume tomorrow morning on the ferry station.

I asked Kitty, "Where are the Ferry Cats going to go? The cats do not have a house, and they make the ferry station a home."

I had to ponder quickly, calculating how much time it would take to save them and still get home before Mr. Bob arrived to feed us.

Kitty and I decided to travel back to tell the cats they were going to lose their home. When we got back, the last ferry for the day was boarding, and we needed to go over to Algiers[*] for the night. I knew of a new shelter for the cat colony to inhabit, so I told them about the construction and we all gathered the food, jumped on the ferry, and rode across the Mighty Mississippi.

When we arrived on the other side, we looked back at the magical, mysterious skyline of New Orleans. The nutria appeared, and Kitty said, "I have missed y'all! Ever since Bone-A-Part's family adopted me I have been living uptown. What's been happenin' on the streets?"

The nutria responded, "No time to talk Kitty; you need to get home because it is getting dark!"

The Ferry Cats, however, had a different idea and dared Kitty and me to take a ride in the pirogue[*] out on the Mississippi River. I said "NO!"

But of course, Kitty didn't listen and went along with what the other cats suggested, and we ended up taking an excursion in the pirogue. This was not my idea of fun, but I went along with the cats.

Thank goodness, the water was smooth and calm; I clearly did not anticipate what would happen next.

As soon as Kitty and I embarked on our short boat ride, the weather suddenly came in and the waves on the Mississippi became violent. I had trouble holding onto the paddle with the boat rocking uncontrollably. Kitty and I hung on to each other for dear life; then the paddle slipped out of my paws, and I watched it float away.

I started to frantically scream "HELP!!!" I had sensed this was a really bad idea and had mistakenly listened to everyone else, especially Kitty. My gut feeling had told me to stay on shore. I did not believe we were going to prevail, but Kitty was nonchalant. We could hear the Ferry Cats from the West Bank.[*] They cheered for us to survive, but the waves were now so large that they were crashing into our small vessel.

The next thing I knew, the nutria had dashed out to our boat and snatched the dangling ropes in the water with their long sharp teeth, towing us through the brutal current. Only then did Kitty realize the danger we were in. Kitty said, "My tail is floating in the boat!" Kitty started to panic because she was a non-swimmer. I naturally and instinctually could swim dog paddle, so I was not as traumatized, but Kitty was now frozen with fear.

Unfortunately, the pirogue would not remain intact against the raging waters of the Mississippi. As the boat sank, the nutria, who are excellent swimmers, whisked Kitty to the platform under the bridge, and I dog-paddled after them.

Kitty wailed, "I almost drowned, and I am not getting my fur wet again!"

We were in for a long night. The nutria treaded in the water and kept us company. I now understood why Kitty liked the nutria and appreciated her advice to "not judge a book by its cover." We both felt comforted with their presence and knew the Ferry Cats were safe on the banks of the Mississippi.

We talked all night with the nutria and became fast friends. Their names were Slick, Oscar, and Sonny. (I would later understand that they had answered our S.O.S.[*] call for help.)

Early the next morning, the nutria started to slap their tails and feet in the water. They were trying to get the attention of the tug boat captain who was approaching the bridge. The Ferry Cats started to jump up and down in the most outlandish, quirky ways also. Lou, the senior Ferry Cat, leaped in the water to make a huge splash. All the Ferry Cats meowed, "Get out of the water, Lou![*]"

I felt a chill come over me when I heard this!

Apparently, all of that commotion worked, and the tug boat came toward us. He glanced over and spotted us under the bridge and pulled the tug boat next to the column.

The Captain said, "Now I have seen it all!"

Kitty and I hopped on, and the Captain motored in toward the bank. He radioed ahead for *Robin's Nest* animal rescue to meet us. Slick, Oscar, and Sonny, our new loyal comrades, made sure we arrived safely and said that they were glad we were uninjured. Kitty and I praised them, got off the boat, and boarded the rescue van with the Ferry Cats. At the break of dawn, we were all rescued.

At the rescue, they checked the tags on our collars, and they looked to see if we were microchipped. Then the rescue team immediately contacted Mom.

She rushed down with Mr. Bob, and they both embraced us. She was upset but also relieved. We overheard as we were leaving that the Ferry Cats would be re-homed across the lake and live on a magnificent horse farm. We felt relieved for the cats.

Mom said, "Crescent City Kitty and Bone-A-Part, you have to promise that we stick together as a family and use the buddy system!" We both nodded and lowered our heads.

We went back to Audubon Park that evening and spent time under the Live Oaks with Henry and Faith, our true friends. Kitty and I reflected on the lessons learned and were thankful for the new friends who had helped us.

Crescent City Kitty and I realized that we had many faithful friends in life, both inside and outside of our family.

Le Bon Temps

The End

Glossary

1803 – Year of the Louisiana Purchase from France. This gave control of the Mississippi River and the port of New Orleans to the United States.

Audubon Park – This park was named after artist John James Audubon and opened in 1898.

Algiers (West Bank) – "The Point or Best Bank" is part of Orleans Parish.

Black-bellied Whistling Ducks – A tree duck that whistles.

Bone-A-Part – Napoleon Bonaparte, a French General and Emperor. Legend says that he was to reside in New Orleans after his exile. His death prevented his relocation.

Crescent City – The Mississippi River bends into the shape of a crescent at New Orleans.

Double Yellow-Headed Amazon Parrot – A talkative parrot.

Fly – A park shaped like a butterfly, and part of Audubon Park on the river.

French Quarter – View Carre or Old Square are the original names for this section of New Orleans.

Henry Clay – The Senator known as the "Great Compromiser," he worked in both the House of Representatives and Senate. A Statue of him is in Lafayette Square and a street is named after him in uptown New Orleans.

Jackson Square – Named after General Andrew Jackson. He was a hero in the Battle of New Orleans. The St. Louis Cathedral and Cabildo are also in Jackson Square.

Le Bon Temps – French for "The Good Times."

Lima, Peru – On the Pacific coast and the fourth largest city in Latin America.

Mississippi River – Flows through ten states. Native Americans lived along the river.

Momma and them – Meaning family

Monkey Hill- "Audubon Park Hill," a man-made hill approximately 30 feet above sea level.

MSY- Named after John Bevins Moisant, an American aviator. MSY, is the city code for the Louis Armstrong International Airport in New Orleans.

Nutria – An aquatic rodent that can grow up to twenty lbs.

Parasol – An umbrella

Pirogue – A flat bottom boat used in waterways.

Red-Eared Sliders – A turtle native to Louisiana.

Second Line – A brass band tradition where people dance behind the band.

S.O.S – International distress signal

St. Louis Cathedral – The oldest cathedral in the United States. A Roman Catholic Church in Jackson Square.

Tchoupitoulas Street – A street that runs along the Mississippi River.

Waterloo – Emperor Napoleon Bonaparte was defeated in 1815 in the Battle of Waterloo (Belgium).

WTC – World Trade Center of New Orleans

A story about Homelessness, Hope and Adoption!

Robin and Faith

Boneapart Art, LLC

Made in the USA
Columbia, SC
17 September 2021